PAUL DAVENPORT

SNAKEMAN

Henning Jasper

Illustrations: Bonnie Poulsen

D1726775

nightmare Abstram.

Paul Davenport:
Snakeman
Teen Readers, Level 3

Series editors: Ulla Malmmose
and Charlotte Bistrup

© 2002 by Paul Davenport and
ASCHEHOUG/ALINEA, Copenhagen
ISBN Denmark 978-87-23-90317-4
www.easyreader.dk

Printed in Denmark by
Sangill Grafisk Produktion, Holme Olstrup

BIOGRAPHY

I had the good fortune of being born in a small town (how small? Population 8,500 – well, OK, 8,489) in Northern Maine in the U.S.A. As a boy, my love of fishing led me a merry chase deep into the Maine woods in pursuit of the wily brook trout. Those happy hours instilled in me a love of nature that has remained with me throughout the years. My colleagues can vouch for that. On teacher outings in the lovely German countryside, they know me as the guy who's always interrupting conversations with cries like "Look, there's a hawk!" or "Do you see those deer over there?".

After completing postgraduate work at university in 1975, I moved to Germany, where I have been living – in Lingen (Ems) – and teaching at the same school (a very creative environment) ever since.

I am a regular contributor to journals for teachers of English, have collaborated on an English textbook for German sixth-graders, have written an interactive play for ninth- and tenth-graders, The Royal Choice, and a reader, Wolf Watch, for Teen Readers.

In my spare time I enjoy jogging, playing table tennis and, of course, fishing.

If you want to know if he loves you so, it's in his kiss –
that's where it is – it's in his kiss!

The Shoop Shoop Song (recorded by Cher, 1991)

—

For Chris, for his helpful suggestions

The phonetic transcription in the footnotes follows British English
pronunciation.

1

"So far, so good," Cathy thought with a little grin. She had been playing her part, the part of the "nice girl", well. "They can get to know the real me later. Right now the main thing is to get accepted." This was her third school in the past four or five years, and she knew that it wasn't a good thing to change schools so often. She had read about what often happened to pupils like her: they became outsiders. But she was determined that this wasn't going to happen to her. It was important that she knew about the problem and actively did something about it, instead of just letting things happen. She didn't want to be an outsider. She liked people and she liked being part of the group. But right now she was new at Portland High and no one knew her. So – she would have to work at getting known. She knew from experience how important it was to *make a good impression* right from the beginning.

The school day had begun well. The homeroom teacher, Mr. Deedles, had *set the right tone*. Before the day's classes got started he had talked to her personally and asked her whether she would like him to introduce her to the class or would she prefer to introduce herself. She had let him do it. That fit in better with the kind of good-girl image of herself she was trying to present.

She had smiled sweetly as he told the class all the nice things she had told him about herself. When some of the pupils wanted to know more, she answered their questions in a quiet way.

---

to make a good impression: to make people think highly of you
to set the right tone: to create a good atmosphere

As soon as the bell rang, one of the boys hurried over to her. With his good looks and warm smile, he had caught Cathy's eye when he first walked in the room. Standing in front of her now, he looked even better.

5   "Hello, Cathy. My name is Jamie Hanson. I write for the school newspaper. We'd like to do an interview with you. Is that alright?" Hey, he's well-mannered, not pushy like a typical reporter. Is he acting, too?

   "Sure. But I don't have much time."

10   "How about during lunch? It won't take long. I already have what Dee-Dee said about you."

   "Dee-Dee?"

   "Mr. Deedles. I'll meet you in front of the cafeteria door after the Biology class, okay?"

15   "Okay."

   Cathy was trying to think of something to say, but Jamie *spun around* and was off. She stood there a minute following him with her eyes. Her face felt a little warm. Then she took a quick look at her *schedule* before mov-
20 ing out into the flow of pupils in the *corridor*.

   The morning went by quickly. She liked most of her new teachers, especially the funny little Spanish teacher, Mr. Ferrero, whose English was so ...well, Spanish, and her Chemistry teacher, the attractive Ms.
25 McPherson wasn't bad either. It was fun watching her *put* the big boys *in their place*, showing them who was boss in the classroom, although she wasn't that much older than her pupils. She didn't like her math teacher,

---

to spin around: to turn around very quickly
schedule: ['ʃedjuːl] timetable
corridor: ['kɒrɪdɔː] hall
to put sb in their place: to criticize sb when they behave badly

Mr. Arnold, but that probably had less to do with Mr. Arnold, who was really quite friendly, than with the fact that she couldn't stand math.

The interview with Jamie was fun. He didn't do it the way most reporters do, *mechanically*, reading from a list of ready-made questions. Instead, he picked up things she said and asked her about them, so that one question led easily to another. It all seemed so natural. Like when he asked her about her hobbies and she said riding, he wanted to know if she was going to join the local riding club, or when she said that she liked to read, he asked her what books she had enjoyed most in the past few months. He asked her a lot of questions about reading. Apparently, it was a hobby of his, too. When he asked her if she'd like to work for the school newspaper, her heart beat faster, but she put a serious look on her face and said she'd have to think about it. She said that she'd like to, but that she was very busy, the school was new and there was so much to get used to, etc. etc. At the end of the lunch hour, Jamie said that he had enough material for his article and thanked her. Before he left he *reminded* her to think about working for the newspaper and she said that she would. Of course she would, she thought, and she would also think about how nice it would be working with Jamie and getting to know him better. But she didn't say that.

mechanically: like a machine
to remind: to help sb remember sth important

2

When the final bell rang the pupils jumped up and hurried out of the classrooms. Almost all of them, including Cathy, were heading for their *lockers* before leaving the school for the day. Before she could find
5 hers, most of the other pupils were already on their way out. Cathy had just opened her locker when she felt an *unpleasant* presence behind her, as if a dark shadow had fallen on her. She took out her jacket and turned around slowly. What she saw made her heart take a
10 jump, but she tried to act as naturally as possible. He was tall and thin, with the small head and hard, empty eyes of a snake. He was smiling, but his smile was not at all friendly. He didn't say anything at first. He just stared at her. She also noticed two other boys, both of
15 them with black boots and short hair, standing a few feet away on either side of her.

"Where are all those friendly pupils now," she thought, looking up and down the corridor for someone from her class. But of the few pupils still there,
20 there was no one she recognized. "Uh, hello. My name is Cathy Crosby, I'm new at the school." She laughed a short, nervous laugh. She went back to the role that had worked so well for her throughout the day.

"I know who you are. Your name is already on my
25 list."

"List? What list?"

"It's a list of members, members of my club." He pulled

---

locker: a small cupboard that can be locked
unpleasant: [ʌnˈplezənt] not nice, unfriendly

a booklet from his pocket, opened it, and *flashed* a list of names in front of her face.

"You're wrong about that. I didn't sign up for any club," Cathy said looking him straight in the eye.

5 "That's OK. I signed for you. Let me explain the rules of the club. We meet right here once a week, same time, same place. The meetings are short. You hand over the money and I make a note of your payment. Got it?" He *hissed* the words at her, his tongue

10 *darting* in and out. His eyes were thin lines.

"I don't understand. Payment, what payment? For what?"

"I just told you. You're in the club. You have to pay membership *dues*, weekly dues."

15 Cathy grinned in his face. "What if I don't want to be in your so-called club?"

He threw back his head and gave a loud laugh, but stopped suddenly and took a step closer to her. He was standing very close to her now. The strong smell of

20 *nicotine* filled her nose.

"That was a dumb question. I'll say it once more. You're already in the club. Now shut up and pay up!"

This situation wasn't new to Cathy. It was common in the inner-city schools she had come from. "And

25 how much are the dues?" she asked in a cool voice.

"Five dollars a week. Nothing to get *upset* about."

---

to flash: to show sth quickly
to hiss: to make a sound like a long 's'
to dart: to move suddenly and quickly
dues: money paid for being a member of a club, etc.
nicotine: ['nɪkəti:n] a kind of drug contained in cigarettes
upset: unhappy

"Well, I am upset, snake-face, so you'd better just *piss off* before I get angry and start screaming." Cathy's dark eyes flashed a warning.

"Hey, boys, did you hear that? She's not only good-looking, she's *tough*, too. I like that, I really do." He turned back to Cathy. "But if there's one thing I hate, it's when people don't show me respect. I'm afraid I'm going to have to teach you what that means – RESPECT." He *seized* her arms and threw her back up against the locker. He pushed his face into hers and laughed. That was when Cathy brought up her knee hard between his legs. She had expected him to cry out, but she was the one who cried. She had struck something *solid*, hard as a rock.

"Oh, didn't I tell you? I always wear my *cup* when I'm on the job. I used to be a *catcher*," he cried, laughing wildly.

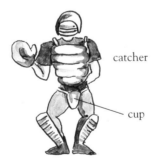

catcher

cup

---

piss off (slang, rude): go away immediately!
tough: [tʌf] strong, not easily defeated
to seize: [siːz] to take hold of sth quickly and firmly
solid: firm, hard
cup: a piece of equipment worn between the legs for protection by a catcher (baseball)
catcher: in baseball, the player who stands behind the batter

11

Pain shot through her knee and ran down her leg. Laughing louder now, he pressed her arms harder. Looking into those cold, empty eyes, Cathy suddenly felt *weak* and leaned back against the locker for sup-
5 port.

"You're in the big league here, *sweetie*, so listen and listen good! *Cooperation* is the magic word. You have to learn to cooperate. If you cooperate with me, everything will be alright. But if you don't cooperate, if you don't
10 show up for our 'meetings' for any reason, or if you try to get help – from other pupils or teachers or whatever – you'll be sorry. I repeat: you'll be sorry. I have friends in this school, lots of friends, some of them in high places, and they report everything they see and hear to me. Big
15 Brother is watching you. So don't do anything stupid or I'll be forced to hurt you." He took her face in his hands and *rubbed* her skin. "You wouldn't want anything to happen to that pretty face of yours, would you? Or...," he grinned, "to Mike?"
20 " Mike?" Cathy's eyes widened.

"You know who I mean. Your little brother."

"But how...?"

"I told you: I've got friends. They're everywhere. I know about everything that goes on in this school. But
25 not to worry. Nothing will happen to you or your dear brother as long as you remember what I told you about the golden rule: COOPERATION!"

He was pressing against her now, the cold touch of his skin sending shock waves down her back. Suddenly, he

weak: not physically strong
sweetie (slang): dear
cooperation: willingness to do as you're told
to rub: to move your hand over sth, while pressing down

pushed her away from him and held out his hand. "First payment!" Cathy said nothing. She put her hand in her pocket and pulled out a five dollar bill. He seized it, turned, gave a little signal to the other two, and hurried away. Cathy stood there a minute or two, breathing ⁵ deeply and rubbing her knee.. Then she closed her locker and walked slowly down the long, nearly empty corridor to the main door.

3

On her way home in the schoolbus Cathy was like a *zombie*. She stared straight ahead of her, but didn't see ¹⁰ anything. Her eyes were turned within, on the scene that had taken place in the school just a few minutes before. It was playing like a film in her head. Some of the pupils in the bus noticed her strange behavior, but they didn't feel they knew her well enough to talk with ¹⁵ her. Besides, it looked like she didn't want to talk.

"Hey, Cath, how was your first day at the new school?" Mike said when she came into the kitchen.
    Cathy was ready for Mike's question and she knew exactly what her answer would be. "Not bad, I guess. I ²⁰ spent most of the morning trying to find out where I was supposed to be. It wasn't easy at first, but I was finding my way quite well after a while. I actually got to some of my afternoon classes on time. Most of my teachers are okay. One or two were a little strange. But ²⁵

zombie: ['zɒmbɪ] a person who seems only partly alive, with no interest in what is happening around them

13

that's the same in every school, isn't it? I'll just have to get used to them."

She checked Mike's reaction to make sure he hadn't noticed that she was hiding something from him. Good, a normal reaction, he's only half listening, she thought.

"And your first day?"

"Not bad. The kids in my class were nice, the teachers, too, except for our *phys ed* teacher. He must have come straight from the army, a former *drill sergeant* or something like that. He took us to the track outside and said he wanted to test our condition. We had to keep running until we almost *dropped*. One of the boys did *pass out*, but do you think he let us stop? No, he just pulled the boy out of the way and told us to keep going." Between sentences, Mike was busy shoving a large sandwich into his mouth and washing it down with a liter of milk that he was drinking straight from the bottle. Mike was a *bottle* man. No cups or glasses for him; they were too small. Finishing quickly, he moved for the door.

"Where are you off to?"

"To the park to play some basketball. See you later."

"See you." Cathy stood in the doorway and smiled as she watched her 'little' brother jump on his bike and ride off. If he keeps growing the way he is now he'll be

phys ed: short for physical education (sport)
drill sergeant: ['drɪl ˌsɑːdʒənt] the one who trains soldiers to perform military actions
to drop: to fall down
to pass out: to lose consciousness for a short time
bottle: a glass container, especially for drinks

ready for the NBA soon, she thought. She was happy to see Mike go. She wanted to be alone with her thoughts.

In the two hours until her mother would return from work, there was one question Cathy would have to try to answer: to tell or not to tell. Usually, she told her mom everything, but she wondered whether it was the right moment to talk about her big problem. She knew that Eileen had been under a lot of pressure in connection with their move. Her new position – manager of the new *branch* of the computer company she worked for – would certainly not be easy at first. Maybe it would be better to wait a few days until she got used to her new job.

It was late when her mom finally came home. Cathy listened *patiently* to her talk about some of the problems she had had on her first day at her new job, but then told her that she had to finish her homework Eileen thought she looked *pale* and told her to lie down first. Cathy said she would and hurried off to her room.

When she got there she turned on her lamp and spread some books on her desk, just *in case* her mother looked in. Then she sat cross-legged on the floor with her back against the wall, her favorite position when she had some deep thinking to do. She spent the next

NBA: National Basketball Association
branch: a local part of a large company
patiently: waiting a long time without becoming angry
pale: when the skin is whiter because of illness, shock, etc.
in case: because of the possibility of

two hours there, her body very still but her mind moving quickly. Many thoughts raced through her head, ideas about how she could deal with her *enemy*. She thought through each of them. In the end she nodded
5 her head. She had hit on the strategy she thought would be best – at least in the beginning, until she had the chance to look around and get to know her new school better.

4

The next few weeks when the Snakeman – Cathy's pri-
10 vate name for him – came for his money, she just handed it over to him. She had decided that *for the time being* a strategy of *non-resistance* would be the best and, in fact, it seemed to be working well. He came, took the money and moved on. But after a while, Cathy began
15 to notice a change. It was the strange way he looked at her, as if he wanted her to say or do something. "Maybe I'm making his work too easy for him," she thought. "Maybe he would prefer more action."

The next time he came around she handed him the
20 money as usual, but instead of turning away, he continued staring at her. Cathy stared back.

"Nice *necklace* you've got there. Where did you get it?" he said, pulling on it playfully.

---

enemy: ['enəmɪ] a person who hates sb or who speaks or acts against them
for the time being: for a short time
non-resistance: not fighting against or trying to stop
necklace: ['nekləs] a piece of jewelry worn around the neck

"I've had it since I was a little girl," Cathy lied. "It isn't real."

"Then you won't mind giving it to me – as a sign of our friendship." He laughed when he said this, but he was waiting to see her reaction.

"In that case, I'd rather keep it," she said coolly.

necklace

"Tell you what. I'll take it with me and have a friend of mine take a look at it. He's an expert on these things. He can tell us whether it's real or not."

"And then you'll bring it back to me. Is that the idea? Should I hold my breath until you do?"

"Now, now, have you already forgotten what I said about respect and cooperation? Or do I have to remind you again? Are you going to hand over the necklace like a nice girl or am I going to have to take it?" He began to pull on it harder.

"No, wait, please!" She reached behind her neck and took off the necklace. He seized it and shoved it into his pocket before disappearing in the crowded corridor.

A feeling of anger struck Cathy. What was wrong with her? He had taken her *valuable* necklace, the one her mom had given her on her last birthday, and she had let him. She had practically given it to him!

Home again, she thought long and hard about what to

valuable: very important

17

do. One thing was certain: she wasn't going to just hand over the money any more. The strategy of non-resistance had failed. She had to try something else. But what? Suddenly, the phone rang.

5   "Cathy? This is Jamie. You remember me asking you about working for the school newspaper? Have you thought about it? We'd really like to have you on the team. Besides, one of our reporters is sick and will be out for a long time, and we need help."

10   "I don't know. I'm so busy." Cathy knew she'd say yes, but she enjoyed talking with Jamie and it was fun *playing* her old game of *hard to get*.

"Oh, come on, Cath, please. The *guys* on the team are great."

15   "Yeah, who are they? Is there anyone I know?"

"There's Jesse and Ophir from our class and three or four others you probably don't know – but they're nice, too. You'd like them."

In the end Cathy agreed to join the group on a 'try-
20 out' basis. She would come to one or two meetings and if she liked it, she would stay. Jamie was *delighted*.

It was hard to get back to her thoughts about the Snakeman after talking with Jamie, but her new *Travis* CD helped her to concentrate again. After a while she
25 realized what her next step would be: she would take a hard look around the school and search for people, pupils or teachers, she felt she could trust. She realized that she couldn't beat her enemy alone, he was too

---

to play hard to get: to make yourself more attractive by acting as if you aren't interested
guy (infl AE): man or woman
delighted: very pleased
Travis: pop group

18

strong. She needed help. But she would have to be careful about which people she talked to. He had friends, lots of friends, not just among the pupils but also "in high places", he had said.

5

"How high?" Cathy asked herself as she waited outside the principal's office. "Is it possible...no, don't even think it, Cathy, it's not possible." She had watched Dr. Callahan closely the past few days, trying to *size* him *up*. In his speech at the beginning of the year he had said that this was his final year at Portland High, and emphasized that he was looking forward to a very successful year – a "perfect year", as he put it, so that he could leave the school after twenty years of service with a feeling of *pride* in a job well done. And then he had gone on about wanting all the pupils of Portland High to consider him their friend, about his office being always open, and about his wish that pupils should feel free to come to him at any time with their questions or problems, etc. etc. Still, there was something about the man that made Cathy unsure. Was it because he always seemed to be in such a big hurry? For one who said *communication* was very important, he didn't seem to have the time to do that much communicating. But maybe it was different inside his office,

---

to size sb up: to form an opinion or a judgement about sb
pride: a feeling of pleasure or satisfaction because you've done sth good
communication: giving information to others

when you had an appointment with him. "Ms. Crosby, the principal will see you now." The secretary smiled at her and pointed to the door.

Dr. Callahan stood up when she came in, asked her
5 to have a seat and waited until she sat down before sitting back down himself.

"Well, well, Cathy Crosby from New York," he said. "How do you like it way up north here in the state of Maine?"

10 When Cathy said she liked it and added that she was the *outdoor type*, Dr. Callahan was suddenly all smiles. He asked her about her love of the outdoors and then went on for the next several minutes about his summer home on the coast where he went as often as possible,
15 especially when the weather was right for sailing. He loved sailing. "After this year," he said with a happy smile, "my wife and I will be spending all our time there."

The appointment lasted about fifteen minutes. It
20 started with small talk and ended with more small talk. Dr. Callahan seemed friendly, but behind his friendly manner there was something about him that warned Cathy not to say what was on her mind. Even when she had only hinted at her problem, he had started pulling
25 at his *tie* and *clearing* his *throat* nervously. What was making him so nervous? Was it just the pressure connected with running a very large high school, was it the

---

Ms.: [mɪz] used before a woman's name when you are speaking to her, if you don't know or don't want to state whether she is married or not
outdoor type: the kind of person who likes to be outside
tie: a long narrow piece of cloth worn around the neck, esp. by men
to clear your throat: to cough so that you can speak clearly

things he had said about wanting his final year to be a very good year for Portland High, or was it ...? No, no, it couldn't be, could it? Whatever it was, Cathy left the principal's office with the certain feeling that she couldn't talk with Dr. Callahan about the Snakeman and his gang.

tie

bat

6

As she went through the school in the days that followed, Cathy thought of herself as Batwoman. Like a *bat* she was sending out signals and picking them up when they came *bouncing* back to her. She searched the faces of pupils and teachers, she listened carefully to what they were saying and observed the body language that went with it. It wasn't long before she had made a kind of mental list. There were three categories of pupils and teachers: those she felt she could trust, those she couldn't trust and those she wasn't sure about. High on the list of those she thought she could trust was Mr. Black, one of the *counselors*. She decided to start with him.

bat: a small flying animal that looks like a mouse
to bounce back: to move back quickly
counselor: ['kaʊnsələ] a person trained to advise people with problems

21

"Let's see, here it is: Cathy Crosby." Looking at his computer, Mr. Black had found her name in the class lists and looked up at her with smiling, interested eyes. "What's your problem, Cathy?"

5   Cathy had thought about what she would say. Although she felt sure that Mr. Black would be on her side, she had decided to be careful. "I don't want to disappoint you, Mr. Black, but I don't have a real problem, at least not a big one." Cathy searched his eyes. She

10   thought she noticed a *trace* of *impatience*.

"Well, let's see if I can help you with your little problems," he said laughing. "And call me Hal, please."

Hal's professional smile disappeared when Cathy started talking about the differences between her pre-

15   sent school and the school she had gone to before, and explaining how difficult it was to get used to the changes. "For example, the classrooms are much further apart than they were in my old school. It's not always easy to get to the next class on time. And some

20   of the teachers aren't at all nice about that. They close the door as soon as the bell rings and if you come in after that, they look at you as if you were from Mars. They know that I'm new here, but they seem to expect me to *function* just as well as everyone else." When the

25   counselor remained silent, Cathy added "I don't think that's right, do you, Hal?" She looked at him expectantly.

"Hmmm," was all Hal said.

Cathy was surprised at how different Mr. Black was

trace: a very small amount of sth
impatience: unwillingness to wait long
to function: to work in the correct way

in the counseling situation. In the cafeteria, where he often sat with pupils, he seemed easy-going and friendly. But now he was giving her the feeling that she shouldn't be wasting his time with such unimportant things. Nevertheless, she pushed on, *steering* the con- 5 versation to the point where she would find out what she wanted to know about him.

"Is there a lot of stealing in the school?" she asked.

"Why do you ask?" He leaned forward and put his elbows on the desk. 10

"Because…my necklace was stolen." Cathy focused on his reaction.

"Stolen? Are you sure? How did it happen?" A worried look filled his eyes.

"I'm not sure. I think it happened during phys ed. I 15 left it in my equipment bag and when class was over it was gone."

"Did you report it to the principal's office?" He fixed her with his worried eyes.

"No, I came to you. That's why I'm here." 20

"Okay, alright, good!" The relief was written all over his face. "I'll be glad to look into it for you, Cathy. Of course, you mustn't get your hopes up. School *thieves* are hard to catch. In fact, they usually get away with it." I'm sure they do, Cathy thought. "Just a second," he 25 said, pressing a button on his computer. He waited a moment, then pressed another button. "Okay, go ahead, tell me all the details."

Cathy went through the rest of her story quickly. She knew what she had come to find out. Before she 30

to steer: to control so that sth goes in the direction you want it to
thief (thieves): a person who takes things belonging to others

left his office, Cathy had already crossed Mr. Black off the list of those she could trust.

7

Cathy felt that the time was right. Eileen was having her after-supper-cup-of-coffee and seemed to be more
5 relaxed than she had been in weeks.

"Mom? You know what I told you about my necklace – that it was stolen at school?"

"Yes. But don't worry about it, dear. I'll get you one to replace it, just like the one you had." Eileen smiled
10 warmly.

"Wait, Mom. The time has come to tell you the whole truth about what happened to the necklace. It was stolen, but not the way I told you." Cathy saw the worried look on her mother's face, so she hurried on.
15 "There's a guy at school who goes around *extorting* money from pupils and I'm on his list. He's the one who took the necklace."

"Oh, my God!" Eileen put down her cup.

"I've been talking with a lot of pupils, trying to find
20 out more about him. Two of the pupils I spoke with, one of them a *junior* and the other a *freshman*, told me that they were on his list, too. They didn't want to talk about it at all at first, but when they realized that they could trust me they opened up and told me everything.
25 The junior has been on his list for a year already, the

to extort: to make sb give you sth by using threats
junior (AE): a pupil in the year before last at high school
freshman (AE): a pupil in the first year at high school

freshman, like me, is new to the list. Both of them are very afraid of him. They told me that the only way they can deal with the situation is by giving him what he wants and not saying anything about it. They made me promise not to use their names when talking about ₅ this. One of them, the girl, said that she had *learned* her *lesson* the hard way. When he found out that she had been talking with other pupils about him, he *punished* her. She showed me the marks on her back."

"Oh, Cath, why didn't you tell me about this ₁₀ before?" Eileen reached over and took Cathy's hand.

"I thought I could handle the problem by myself. I had to deal with the same thing in my last school, remember? Besides, you were just starting your new job here and you had enough problems of your own. I didn't ₁₅ want to add to them."

Eileen was shaking her head. "That was sweet of you, Cath, but wrong. My problems are nothing compared with yours. You shouldn't have waited with this. Have you at least talked to a teacher or the principal about ₂₀ it?"

"It's not that simple, Mom. He isn't alone. He's the head of a gang and he says he's got a lot of pupils and even teachers on his side. He threatened to hurt me or Mike if I don't cooperate with him." ₂₅

Eileen gave a little *gasp* and *squeezed* her eyes shut. She seemed to be imagining what could happen to her children. When she finally spoke, her words came slowly. "And you've been keeping all this to yourself?

to learn your lesson: to realize what must be done
to punish: to make sb suffer because they have done sth wrong
gasp: a short quick breath of air when you are surprised or in pain
to squeeze: to press firmly from two sides

You're a strong girl, Cathy, stronger than I thought. What can we do?"

"I thought I knew how to deal with it. I played it cool and gave him his money. But it didn't work. He wanted more. That's when he took the necklace. And last week he noticed that I wasn't wearing my *watch*. I said I had lost it, but he knew I was lying. He wants me to bring it with me the next time. He seemed to read my thoughts. I was thinking of bringing a cheap one instead, but he said no tricks, he wants the original watch. He knows exactly what kind it is."

"But Cathy, that watch is worth over a hundred dollars."

"You asked me what we can do. Well, what I'm doing is looking for people I can trust. I can't fight this thing alone, I'm not Lara Croft, I need help."

"Lara who?"

"Never mind, Mom."

"Well, I'll help you. But how? Shall I talk to some of the parents?" Eileen was talking very quickly as she always did when she got nervous.

"Not yet, Mom. I think it would be better to find out which of the pupils and teachers are on our side first. We need a base – a team. But we have to act carefully. The Snakeman – that's what I call him because he reminds me of a snake – means it when he says he's got people *spying* for him everywhere in the school and when he says he will hurt me or Mike if I don't cooperate with him."

At Cathy's last words, Eileen gasped again and put

watch: a small clock worn on the wrist
to spy: to watch secretly

26

her hands over her face. "Oh, Cath, you think he'd really do that? Shouldn't we call the police?"

"Not yet, Mom. it's too soon for that. I need time, time to gather information and find people who'll help us. Don't worry. I'll be careful. I won't give him any rea- son to hurt me or Mike, I promise." There was that look of determination on Cathy's face that Eileen knew so well. She looked lovingly at her daughter, unable to decide between her motherly instinct to protect her and her wish to respect Cathy as a young woman with a need to be responsible for her own actions. Finally, she got up and went around the table. She stood behind her daughter a moment without saying anything, then she placed a hand on her back.

"OK, Cath, you do it your way, but remember, I'm on your side. If there's anything I can do to help, you can depend on me."

"Thanks, Mom. That helps a lot – just knowing that you're behind me." Cathy looked up and smiled.

"What about Mike? Have you told him?"

"Not yet. Do you think we should?" Cathy empha- sized the 'we' to show Eileen that she was part of her team now.

"No, I don't. I think it would be too hard on him, don't you? Of course, if things change and the Snake- man finds out what you *are up to*, we'll have to warn Mike at once."

"That's exactly what I was thinking," Cathy said. She got up and put her arms around her mother. "It'll be alright, Mom. We'll get through this." They stood there several minutes, holding each other tight.

| *to be up to sth*: to be secretly doing sth

27

8

So Cathy continued working on her 'list'. After Mr. Black, she had decided to concentrate on her classmates and her own teachers. In the weeks that followed she became very good at testing how far she could trust others. The list of people she felt she could talk with openly was growing. But in the past few days, she had slowed down. There was less pressure. The situation with the Snakeman had improved. He came, took his money and left. Now that he had her necklace and watch, he seemed to be *satisfied* for the time being. Besides, the work with the school newspaper had become very interesting. The others all told her that she was good at writing and it was exciting seeing her name in print. Also, the weekly staff meetings were a lot of fun, especially because Jamie always seemed to have a reason to work closely with her. Somehow, they often had to stay longer than the others. Of course, there were a lot of things about newspaper writing he had to teach her, and she was a very willing pupil.

When he asked her if she would like to go canoeing with him on the river, she was delighted. She loved the great outdoors. But, *true to form*, she said she'd never been in a canoe, never had a paddle in her hand , etc. etc. In the end she agreed to be ready early the next morning when he came to pick her up.

What a day that was! A day for the Guinness Book of Records, a day of surprises and *superlatives* – that's

satisfied: happy
true to form: behaving in a typical way
superlative: [suːˈpɜːlətɪv] the biggest, highest, best, etc. of anything

how she described it in her *diary*.

On their way out of the city in the *pickup* Jamie's dad had let him have for the day, Cathy listened with apparent interest to Jamie telling her how to handle a canoe. She didn't say that she already knew how to 5
canoe. Later, out in the river, he was surprised at how much she had learned and he told her what a good canoeist she was already. They had started out well, moving quickly over the dark water, but they hadn't gone far when they heard the first angry sounds in the 10
distance.

pickup

"Oh, oh. Bad storm on its way," Jamie shouted. "But it's going to miss us, I think." Famous last words. Shortly after, the sky turned black, and the storm was suddenly upon them. The *lightning* flashed in the darkness 15
and the *thunder crashed* around them. They were racing

lightning

diary: ['daɪərɪ] a book you can use to write down your thoughts and experiences of each day
pickup: a small truck with low sides and no roof at the back
lightning: a flash in the sky caused by electricity
thunder: a loud noise after a flash of lightning
to crash: to make a loud noise

to safety when lightning struck a tree at the edge of the river just beyond them, turning it into a ball of fire. When they *panicked* the canoe got out of control, and before they realized what had happened, it had turned
5 over and both of them were in the water. It was a good thing they had on *life jackets*. Eileen had made them promise to wear them. Still, the icy-cold water was a shock to Cathy. When she shot to the surface, she saw Jamie holding onto the canoe and signaling to her to
10 help him pull it to *shore*. The shore wasn't that far away, but when they finally reached it they were out of breath. There they lay, like *stranded* fish, breathing heavily, while the storm passed over them. When they had rested long enough, they *waded* into the river and
15 began to search for the stuff that had fallen out of the canoe when it turned over. Half an hour later they had found most of it, including Jamie's *fishing rod*. By that time, they were both hungry, and Jamie used his rod "moving it like a *magic wand* over the water" (com-
20 ment in her diary) to catch the fish she cooked for their meal.

Looking back on it, what happened next was the best part of the trip. After they had eaten they hung their wet clothes next to their campfire to dry. They
25 stood as close to the fire as they could trying to get

---

to panic: to suddenly feel so frightened that you cannot think clearly
life jacket: a jacket filled with air so you can float in the water
shore: the land along the edge of a river, lake, etc.
stranded: left in a place from which you can't leave
to wade: to walk slowly through water
fishing rod: a long stick with a fishing line and hook, used for catching fish
magic wand: a thin stick held by sb when doing magic tricks

warmed up. But the time spent searching in the ice-cold water had *chilled* them *to the bone*. Then Jamie hit on the idea of giving each other a *massage* to get the blood moving again. "A cool idea" was how Cathy described it in her diary.

Jamie began, and he worked hard, his strong fingers doing their magic, driving the cold out of Cathy's body. Then it was Cathy's turn and she concentrated on doing her best at first, but after a few minutes she decided that she would rather have a little fun. She began to *tickle* Jamie, just a little at first, so that he wasn't sure whether she was tickling or massaging. Then, before he realized what was happening, she became a tickle machine. Jamie tried to shake her off, but she stuck to him like a rodeo rider to a wild horse. Besides, all the tickling was making him weak. He rolled over and over, laughing uncontrollably. When she stopped and he was able to gain control of himself again, he was looking for *revenge*. He ran after her up and down the shore until she fell onto the sand. Not far behind her, he threw himself down and moved slowly across the sand toward her like some kind of *creepy-crawly* monster, making strange monster noises. She was already shaking with laughter before he even touched her, but when he started tickling her, she went into *hysterics*. After a while, the laughter was hurting her so much

---

to chill to the bone: to make very cold
massage: ['mæsɑːʒ] rubbing a person's body to reduce pain, etc.
to tickle: to touch a sensitive part of sb's body to make them laugh
revenge: sth you do to make sb suffer because they have made you suffer
creepy-crawly (infl): [ˌkriːpɪ'krɔːlɪ] an insect, worm, etc. when you think of it as unpleasant
hysterics (infl): [hɪ'sterɪks] wild laughter

that she *begged* him to stop. When he finally did, it took her several minutes to get her breath back. What had begun in a quiet, serious way had ended in a happy *free-for-all*. In her diary she wrote: TICKLE PARTY!
5 And: the best place to tickle Jamie =the neck.

After a while they were out on the river again, paddling along, taking in the fascinating sights, sounds and smells of the countryside around them. There were flowers of all shapes and colors, their sweet smells
10 everywhere. There were birds Cathy had never seen before, fantastic-looking birds, their songs filling the air. There were animals in the water: *turtles*, *beavers* and the fast-moving *otters*. And animals on land: rabbits, *racoons* and the light-footed *deer*. And there were fish,
15 dark shapes darting away through the water like shadows when the canoe came near.

beaver

turtle

"*Garden of Eden*," cried Cathy, half-turning so Jamie could hear her better.

"That's Maine! I thought you'd like it," Jamie cried
20 back.

to beg: to ask for sth in a very strong or serious way
free-for-all: a situation with no rules or controls
deer (pl. deer)
Garden of Eden: the beautiful garden where Adam and Eve first lived

The highlight of the afternoon wasn't planned, it came as a big surprise. They had just come around a sharp turn when they almost ran into two *moose*. There they stood, two long-legged *giants*, both with their heads under water, feeding. Jamie shoved his paddle deep into ⁵ the water, slowing them down. He signalled to Cathy

deer

racoon

otter

moose

and she helped him steer the canoe in behind a tree next to the water. It was a good hiding place. They sat there for the next half hour, fascinated at the sight of those *majestic* creatures. When they had seen enough, ¹⁰

moose (pl. moose)
giant: ['dʒaɪənt] unusually large creature
majestic: [mə'dʒestɪk] impressive because of size or beauty

they paddled out quietly from behind the tree in order not to upset them. They didn't. In fact, the moose hardly looked up as the canoe came towards them. But

Cathy felt *goose pimples* – "moose pimples", she wrote later in her diary – break out all over her as they sailed by, not more than a few yards away, almost close enough to reach out and touch them.

Later, on their way back, they were moving in the direction of the setting sun, an *explosion* of reds and yellows, as if they were paddling straight into a painting by Van Gogh. When they had pulled the canoe out of the water and put it onto the pickup, they stood there for what seemed like a long time, holding hands, just staring at the sky. Cathy had felt close to Jamie that day, like part of a team, but the feeling of closeness she had now was even stronger, like the colors that surrounded them. When she suddenly turned and said something in his ear, Jamie took her in his arms and kissed her.

As she finished her description of the day in her diary, she was writing and singing at the same time: "If you want to know, if he loves you so, it's in his kiss!"

9

There was something different about the Snakeman this time. Cathy noticed it at once. It was the way he was looking at her.

"Have you ever thought about getting *tattooed?*" he asked suddenly.

---

goose pimples: raised spots on your skin because you feel cold, frightened, etc.
explosion: the sudden loud noise when a bomb, etc. goes off
(to get) tattooed: [tə'tuːd] to have a picture marked on your skin

"I've thought about it, yes," Cathy said carefully, surprised at the personal question.

"And...?"

"And I'm still thinking about it. I haven't made up my mind yet."

"I think a tattoo would look good on you. Maybe something like this!" He started taking off his shirt.

"Forget it. I don't want to see your tattoo," Cathy said, turning her head away.

But he didn't seem to hear her. He opened the shirt wide. "How do you like this?" He grinned at her.

Cathy couldn't help herself. She had to stare at the tattoo, a huge *dragon* breathing fire and looking very dangerous. And when he moved his *chest* up and down, the dragon came alive, like a *cartoon show*. It was frightening.

dragon

"Yeah, Cath, tattoos are fun. You don't know what you're missing. You should get one. It would look good on you, it really would!" He laughed but his look was serious.

chest: the top part of the front of your body
cartoon show: a movie in which the characters are drawn, e.g. Jungle Book

"What about *choppers*? You ever been on a chopper?" Again that serious look.

"Of course," Cathy lied.

chopper

"What kind?" He was testing her.

"A Hartley." She had heard the name somewhere 5 and hoped she was saying it right.

"Not Hartley, Harley, you mean a Harley Davidson!"

"Yeah, Harley Davidson," Cathy said casually, hoping to cover up her mistake.

"Hey, boys, did you hear that? She's been on a 10 Harley. How'd you like it?" He moved closer to her.

"Oh," she said, forcing herself to smile, "it was fun."

"Well, you're in luck. I got a Harley, one of the biggest. Want to go for a ride with me?"

Cathy realized too late where the conversation was 15 leading. She was *trapped*. She had to find a way out without making him angry.

"I...uh...–" She smiled a quick smile and ran her hand through her hair.

"You're safe with me. I'm a good driver, if that's what 20 you're worried about."

"I...uh...would have to ask my mother." Cathy tried a little girl look.

chopper (AE): a type of motorcycle
trapped: caught in a bad or dangerous situation

37

Mistrustful now, he looked at her hard. "Well, okay, little girl, you ask your *old lady*. I can wait, but I want your answer next week, hear?" He paused to emphasize the importance of his words. "And Cathy... you'd bet-
5 ter *sweet-talk* her, so she'll say yes. You wouldn't want to disappoint me, would you?" His look and his voice had grown hard.

What he meant was perfectly clear.

All the way home, Cathy thought about the change
10 in the Snakeman. She couldn't believe it. He had tak-en a liking to her. It wasn't her money or her jewelry he wanted now – it was her! He wanted her to be his girl! Snakeman's girlfriend! The idea of it almost made her laugh, but when she thought about what a dangerous
15 situation she was now in, she felt more like crying than laughing. She thought and thought until her head felt like it would break apart, but by the time she reached home, she had made a plan. Later, when she went to bed, her head was still hurting.

10

20 "Tighter, hold tighter!"

She did as she was told, *wrapping* her arms tighter around his *waist*.

She didn't see much at first. She was so afraid she kept her eyes closed most of the time, but after a while
25 she got used to the noise and the speed, and started

---

old lady (AE slang): mother
to sweet-talk: talk very nicely to sb (to try to get sth from them)
to wrap: to cover sth in paper or other material

looking around her. They were out of the city now, somewhere in the country. As they rode on there were no more houses to be seen, only a farm here and there. A little later, they came to the woods. It looked dark and dangerous. The sun had disappeared, hidden by 5 the tall trees. As they rode deeper into the woods, it became even darker.

waist

"Enjoying your ride?" he shouted back at her. But instead of waiting for her answer, he gave a wild laugh. "We'll be there soon." 10

Where was "there"? Her mind began to spin and she could see the picture of a dark place in the middle of the woods – was that where he was taking her?

They rode on and on, the woods growing deeper and darker. She felt like screaming, but realized that no one 15 would hear her – no one except him, and he would only laugh his crazy laugh.

Suddenly, they turned into a smaller road. It went up, straight up, higher and higher. Then she remembered: he had said something about a mountain. He 20 would take her to a mountain.

It was a high mountain. She could tell because the air had become thin. It was harder for her to breathe now. As they went higher still, she had to fight for breath. 25

Then they were at the top. He stopped and told her to get off and take off her *helmet*. She did as he said, feeling her panic grow. She felt like running down the mountain as fast as she could, but she could only stand
5 beside the chopper, helpless, her legs like stone. Looking around, she was surprised to see that there were two others there. She didn't recognize them at first – for some reason she couldn't see clearly – but then she realized that it was Dr. Callahan and Mr. Black. She
10 was so happy to see them, but when she called to them for help they just stood there. Couldn't they hear her? What was wrong?

Laughing, he got off the machine, but he left his helmet on. He took her by the hand and led her along
15 a path. She looked back at the two others, but they remained standing where they were. Her heart felt like it would explode. When they reached the edge of the mountain, he turned. "Take a look," he said. She looked down the mountain. The view was exciting.
20 The city they had left a half hour before seemed very near, almost at their feet.

"Can you see the high school?" he asked. Again the crazy laugh.

She turned in the direction he was pointing, *strain-*
25 *ing* her eyes, fighting back her feeling of panic.

"Well?"

"Yes, I see it now," she said.

He started laughing again, louder and louder. Suddenly he stopped. "Portland High. That's my school! I
30 own that school! I'm in control there!" He took her by

helmet: a type of hard hat that protects the head
to strain: to make a great effort to do sth

40

the arm. "You could be part of it, Cathy, you could be my partner! Come on, give me a kiss and we'll be partners." She tried to pull away, but he held her tight.

"It's that Jamie, isn't it? He's the problem."

"Jamie?" she said, as if she had never heard the name 5 before.

"Don't play games with me, Cathy. I know all about you two. I know my school. I know everything that goes on there. Jamie Hanson! The one you went canoeing with. The one you work on the school newpaper 10 with."

She tried to speak, but nothing came out.

"Well, forget about him. He's a loser. I'm the number one at Portland High! Now, come on, Cathy, give me a kiss and show me that you're my girl." With one strong 15 hand he pulled her close, with the other he pulled off his helmet. What she saw made her gasp. It was the head, not of a human being, but of a snake! Screaming, she turned to run, but the snake-like *creature* was faster and caught her by the legs. *Twisting* and turning, she 20 tried to get away but her movements grew weaker and weaker. The creature was wrapping itself slowly but surely around her. She began to shake all over as its ice-cold body pressed on hers. Her heart *pounded* and her breath came short and fast. It had wrapped itself 25 around her whole body now, and was squeezing her tighter and tighter, squeezing the last breath from her body. The last thing she saw before she passed out was the huge mouth of the creature opening wide...

creature: ['kriːtʃə] a living thing such as an animal
to twist: to turn part of your body around while the rest stays still
to pound: to beat quickly and loudly

"Cathy! What's wrong, dear?" Was that Eileen's voice?

"I'm okay, Mom."

"But you were screaming!"

5   "Just a bad dream. I'll be alright."

Shaking her head, Eileen left the room. Cathy lay very still for a long time, waiting for her heart to slow down. Finally, when she could breathe normally again, she sat up in bed. Okay, she thought, that was a dream, a very bad one, but only a dream. The real thing can't ₅ be any worse. You've been in bad situations like that before. You can handle it. Just stick to your plan and everything will be alright.

11

When the *staff* meeting was over and everyone was getting ready to leave, Cathy asked Jamie if he could stay ₁₀ a few minutes and help her with a report she was writing. As soon as the others left, she told him about her problem with the Snakeman, starting from the beginning and ending with what had happened the day before. ₁₅

"I was going to tell you about it before, but I thought I had everything more or less under control, and I didn't want it to get in the way of our friendship."

"But Cathy, that's what friends are for."

"I had a plan. I knew I couldn't fight him alone. He ₂₀ and his organization are too powerful for that. What I wanted to do was find the right people, form a team, and fight him together. But there's no more time for that now. He is forcing me to choose, for him or against him. If I don't agree to go for a ride with him next ₂₅ week, it's hard to say what he will do. But one thing is sure: he'll be very angry with me. And another thing is

staff: group of people working for an organization

43

sure: if I do agree to go with him, it won't end there. He'll want more. He'll think that I'm his girl."

Jamie was listening carefully, his lips pressed close together. "Have you gone to see the principal yet?" he 5 wanted to know.

Cathy nodded. "Yes, but all I got was negative *vibrations*. I don't think he can be trusted."

"You think Dr. Callahan has something to do with this?"

10 "I'm not sure, but I do know he's afraid of it. I got the feeling that he didn't want to know anything about it. You heard his speech, what he said about wanting his last year at Portland High to be perfect and all that."

15 "Have you talked with any of the counselors about it?"

"I spoke with Mr. Black. I had the same feeling I got from Callahan – negative." Surprised at Jamie's silence, Cathy raised her voice. "So what do you think I should 20 do?"

Jamie continued to stare into space a moment. "I...I don't know, Cath. It seems like the Snakeman's got the whole school on his side," he said almost too softly for her to hear.

25 "Maybe he has, but I know a way of finding out for sure."

"You do?"

"Yeah, bring this whole thing out into the open – where it belongs!" Cathy's *fist* hit the table.

vibrations: an atmosphere produced by a person
fist: a hand when it is tightly closed

44

"What do you mean? What are you thinking of?" There was a trace of fear in Jamie's voice.

"Here. Look at this! It's about the Snakeman. You can help me finish it – a front-page story for The Beacon, telling the whole school about him and his gang. It would be hard for Dr. Callahan to continue ignoring the problem if all the pupils were told about what's going on here. It's a chance – our only chance!"

"Uh, huh." Jamie nodded his head slowly. "That's a good idea but there's one problem."

"And that is…?"

"The Beacon doesn't come out until the beginning of next month, two weeks from now. Besides, I'm not sure our *faculty adviser* would approve. She prefers to keep negative things out of the school newpaper."

"Negative things?"

"Yeah, anything that isn't nice. Her idea of Portland High is that of an ideal school, you know, the "wonderful, wonderful world of Portland High", and she tries to keep everything out of The Beacon that doesn't fit in with that idea."

"But what if we talk to her? Couldn't we make her realize how important it is?" Cathy fixed her eyes on Jamie, surprised at his lack of *enthusiasm*.

"Sure, we can talk to her, but I'm warning you: she's a strong person with strong opinions and – I can tell you this from my own experience – it's difficult to get her to change her mind – about anything. So don't get your hopes up too high," he said, smiling weakly. "But

---

faculty adviser: ['fækəltɪ əd'vaɪzə] a teacher whose job it is to help pupils by giving advice
enthusiasm: [ɪn'θjuːzɪæzəm] a strong feeling of excitement and interest

I'll ask her to meet with us. I'll let you know when."
Jamie got up slowly and followed Cathy to the door.

She turned suddenly. "Jamie?"

"Yeah?"

5   "I have strong opinions, too."

"I know you do, Cath," he said softly.

"Hey, come on, Jamie, *be cool*! We're a strong team –
right?" Cathy laughed.

"Right." Jamie tried to laugh, but couldn't.

12

10 The meeting was short. Cathy felt that something was
wrong right from the beginning. Jamie sat next to Ms.
Southerland on one side of the table, and she was alone
on the other. Entering the room, she had got her first
look at Ms. Southerland. She was surprised. She had
15 been expecting a much younger person (because of the
Ms.?), but the gray-haired woman with the long neck
who sat opposite her was old enough to be her grand-
mother. After some nervous small talk, Cathy was
asked to explain her idea about the front-page story in
20 the next *issue* of The Beacon. As she talked Cathy had
a strange feeling, as if she was a criminal and the
woman staring at her from the other side of the table
was a judge. Ms. Southerland didn't say anything the
whole time, she just let her go on talking. When Cathy
25 was finished, Ms. Southerland sat up very straight in
her chair, her head going up and down on her long
neck like an out-of-control bird.

be cool (AE slang): don't get worried or excited
issue: [ˈɪʃuː] one of a regular series

"Those are very serious _accusations_, Cathy," she said. "Do you have any _proof_, anything that would stand up in court?" She evens talks like a judge, Cathy thought. Ms. Southerland paused, thrown off balance by the grin on the girl's face. "Don't get me wrong, I believe your story, I really do, but we have to think of what's best for Portland High . If we printed something like this, you can imagine what a _bad light_ it would _cast_ on our school. Did you ever think of that? Do you realize the situation Dr. Callahan and the staff would be put in? Dr. Callahan has been principal of Portland High for almost twenty years. He's been a good principal, good for our high school. This is his final year. Can you imagine the damage your story would cause to his _reputation_ and to the reputation of Portland High?" 5

10

15

Cathy glanced at Jamie, but he looked away quickly. "But it's the truth. Pupils are in danger, our school is in danger. We can't close our eyes to it because of Dr. Callahan or anyone else. We have to do something about it!" Cathy's heart was pounding. 20

"I respect your _concern_, Cathy, but don't you think you are _exaggerating_? You feel perhaps that you are in danger, but that doesn't necessarily mean that the whole school is in danger, does it? We have to be careful not to react too strongly." Ms. Southerland now had 25

accusation: a statement saying that you think a person has done sth wrong
proof: facts that show that sth is true
to cast a bad light on: to make a situation, etc. look bad
reputation: the opinion that people have about what sth or sb is like
concern: a feeling of worry
to exaggerate: [ɪgˈzædʒəreɪt] to make sth seem better, worse, etc. than it really is

a motherly look on her face and her voice was full of understanding.

"React too strongly? I can't believe it. There's a gang out there *terrorizing* our school and all you can say is that we have to be careful. Careful of what, Ms. Southerland?" Cathy cried, her eyes *blazing* with anger.

She turned to Jamie. "Haven't you got anything to say? I thought you were on my side!" she cried.

"I am, Cathy, but Francis – uh, Ms. Southerland has a point. Do we have any real proof to back up these accusations? What could we say when parents want to know the facts? What facts do we have to show them? Sure, you can say that the Snakeman has taken money from you, and *jewelry*, but can you prove it? You're just one person. It's your word against his." Ms. Southerland looked at Jamie proudly.

Cathy *hesitated* a moment, shocked by the way Jamie had spoken, like a *parrot*, repeating what Ms. Southerland had said.

parrot

---

to terrorize: to frighten people so that they will do as they are told
to blaze: to shine brightly
jewelry: ['dʒuːəlrɪ] objects such as rings and necklaces
to hesitate: to be slow to act because you feel uncertain

48

"I told you before: if we exposed this in The Beacon, it would break down this wall of silence. I wouldn't be alone any longer. Other pupils would have the courage to come forward and tell about what the Snakeman has done to them." 5

Ms. Southerland was smiling. "And what if there are no others? What if you're the only one?"

"Listen. The Snakeman keeps a list of his _victims_. There are _dozens_ of names on it. I've seen it with my own eyes." 10

"What if he was only trying to _impress_ you? You said he wants to take you motorcycle riding. Apparently he likes you."

Cathy had had enough. Suddenly, she stood up. Looking angrily at Jamie, she left the room. 15

13

Cathy and Ophir were just finishing off a large pizza when Jamie saw them. Looking unsure of himself, he came over to their table.

"Well...?" He was studying Cathy's face.

"Well what?" she said, giving him a cool look. 20

"Did you go with him?"

"What do you think?" Cathy and Ophir laughed.

"Dressed like that?" Jamie was staring at her tight t-shirt and shorts.

victim: sb who has been hurt or killed by sb else
dozens: ['dʌzənz] a lot of
to impress: to make you think how important sth or sb is

"He liked the way I was dressed," she said with a straight face.

"Hey, what's that?" Jamie's eyes were fixed on her upper arm. His mouth had fallen open. "Isn't that a tattoo?"

Cathy pulled up her *sleeve*. On her upper arm was the picture of a dragon. "Do you like it? I had it done yesterday, in time for my *date* today."

"Yeah, but..." Jamie's ears turned red.

"But what?" 5

"Oh, nothing. I just thought ..." Once again Jamie got stuck and couldn't go on.

Cathy was enjoying this. "You thought...?"

"Forget it. Where did you go?"

"He took me up Bear Mountain." 10

"B-b-b-bear Mountain? But that's over ten miles from here. How long were you there?"

"Hey, what is this, a police report?" The smile on Cathy's face was gone.

"No, no. I didn't mean it to sound like that." 15

"Well, sit down and I'll tell you all about it. We had a lot of fun."

At the word 'fun' Jamie's face twisted. "But Cathy, I don't understand. I thought that I – I mean you and I – I thought that we – ...." He shook his head, unable to 20 go on.

"I know what you mean, Jamie. But that was all before you *let* me *down*, remember?"

"Let you down?"

"Yeah, you and your friend Francis Southerland," 25 Cathy said, looking him in the eye.

"Cathy, can we talk – alone, I mean?"

"It's okay, I was just leaving anyway. Thanks for the

sleeve: a piece of clothing that covers all or part of your arm
date: a meeting with a boyfriend or girlfriend or sb who might become a boyfriend or girlfriend
to let sb down: not to help or support sb as they had hoped

pizza, Cath. It's my turn next time," Ophir said, _winking_ at Cathy as she left the table.

"Well?" Cathy said in a cold tone of voice.

"You know what I think? I think you're using the
5 Snakeman to get back at me for 'letting you down', as you put it. That's a dangerous game you're playing. Besides, I didn't let you down. It was Ms. Southerland, not me, who turned down your idea of using The Beacon as your platform against the Snakeman. I can
10 understand that that was a big disappointment, but it's not fair of you to _take_ it _out on_ me."

"Have you finished? Now I'll tell you what I think. I think that you are a _wimp_, a real wimp. Instead of standing by me, you _sided with_ your friend Francis. You
15 knew I was right, but it was more important to you to please your boss. That's what I call a wimp. But it's alright. In fact, I'm glad it turned out that way. I've got to know Gordon better now – Gordon Baker, that's the Snakeman's real name – , and he's not such a bad guy
20 after all. In fact, we get along quite well together." Cathy leaned back in her chair, a grin on her face.

"But Cathy, you're my girl! Have you forgotten last week on the river already? Have you forgotten what you said to me? Well, I haven't, and I can't believe
25 that you didn't mean it. You're not the type who plays around and hurts people. I know you better than that. You can't be serious about the Snakeman. You can't

---

to wink: to close one eye and open it again quickly, esp. as a signal
to take sth out on sb: to be not nice to sb because you feel angry, hurt, etc., although it is not their fault
wimp (AE slang): a person with a weak character
to side with: to support one person or group against sb else

52

<u>dump</u> me for a guy like that!"

Cathy narrowed her eyes. "You dumped me first."

"What? I dumped you?" Jamie cried.

"You did it when you sided with Ms. Southerland."

"But Cathy, that didn't change my feelings for you," 5
he <u>whined</u>.

"But it changed my feelings for you. You are no longer the Jamie I knew. You became a different person when you did that to me."

Jamie sat very still, his head in his hands. His 10
squeezed his eyes shut and rubbed them, as if he had a headache. Finally, he spoke. "Is there any way we can get back together?" He looked at her through his fingers.

Cathy didn't answer at once. She picked up her *napkin* 15
in her hand and starting twisting it.

Jamie was staring at her. "There is one way," she said slowly, with a strong emphasis on the word 'one'. "You have to go to Ms. Southerland and make her see that she must let us print that story." 20

Jamie gasped, and hid his head in his hands. Cathy continued looking at him. Her expression didn't change. Minutes went by. Suddenly, Jamie stood up and went to the window, his back to Cathy. "And what if I don't?" he said in a whisper. 25

"Then you can consider our relationship as finished. Over and done with – for good! It's as simple as that."

---

to dump sb (infl): to end a friendship
to whine: [waɪn] to say that you are not happy with a situation in a crying voice
napkin: a piece of cloth or paper used at meals to protect your clothes and clean yourself with

Jamie stood perfectly still. He continued to look out the window. "And if I do it?"

"If you do it, and the story gets printed, we can make a fresh start. You have to show me that you're a man, someone I can look up to."

Jamie didn't react at first, as if he hadn't heard Cathy's words. Then, slowly, he began to nod his head. He seemed to be saying something to himself. He came back to the table, sat down, and looked over at Cathy. "I'm going to try," he said.

Without saying anything, Cathy put the napkin in her glass of water and began to rub her tattoo with it. A moment later the tattoo was gone, and the napkin full of colors. "The dragon is dead," she said with a little laugh.

Jamie had to smile.

14

When he sat down beside her in the cafeteria Jamie wasn't smiling. "She said no."

"Just like that?"

"No, not just like that. I argued with her, I *pleaded* with her, but she only looked at me as if I had lost my mind. Then, when I told her that she would have to look for a new *editor-in-chief* if she didn't change her mind, she suddenly changed. She sat down beside me and put her arm around my shoulder. She said I would be crazy to do a thing like that, that I was an excellent

---

to plead: to make an emotional request for sth
editor-in-chief: the person in charge of a newspaper, magazine, etc.

editor – the best she had ever had – and I had a great future ahead of me. She even said that she knew some people who could be useful in my career planning. I think she expected me *to give in* after all that, but when I shook my head and pulled away from her, she started 5 getting loud. She said that I had always been a very sensible and cooperative boy, that she and I had always been such a good team working hand in hand, but that all that had changed when you joined the staff. It was you, she said, who put that crazy idea in my head about 10 the Snakeman. In the end she was shouting. I had never seen her behave like that before. It was shocking."

"So, you Adam, me Eve. It's all my *fault*, is that it?" Cathy gave a bitter little laugh.

"That's her version, but not mine, not any more." 15

"And where does that leave us? Is that the end of the line?"

"No, it's not," said Jamie in a loud voice. "There's another way." He looked around suddenly to make sure no one was listening before continuing. "We'll bring 20 out a special edition of The Beacon – without Ms. Southerland's permission!"

Jamie's words made her heart jump for joy, it was what she had been hoping he'd say. But she had learned to be careful, so she didn't show her feelings at first. It 25 was for her that Jamie had decided to do this, so she had to help him realize what his decision meant.

"Have you thought about the possible consequences? Do you realize that you would probably lose your job as

---

to give in: to agree to do sth you don't want to do
fault: [fɔːlt] if a situation is your fault, you are the cause of it

editor-in-chief of The Beacon and, worse than that, that we might get *suspended* from school?"

"Of course I've thought about it and I realize that we would be taking a big risk, but it's a risk I'm prepared to take." Jamie's hands had turned to fists.

Cathy took his fists in her hands and held them tightly. Her eyes were shining. "I was hoping you'd say that."

15

The next week began like any other at Portland High: bells rang, classes started, classes ended, corridors filled, corridors emptied, teachers taught, and pupils learned – when they weren't busy doing other things.

Nobody noticed that there was a meeting taking place in the room used by the staff of The Beacon. The twelve pupils taking part in the meeting had come to the room one at a time, not as a group, so they wouldn't attract any attention. Six of them were staff members of The Beacon. The other six were taken from Cathy's list of those who could be trusted. She and Jamie had studied that list until they found the right pupils for a special job – as bodyguards! Three of them were football players, two were on the *wrestling* team and one of them was captain of the boxing team. Everybody had been told about the purpose of the meeting, so as soon

suspended: not allowed to go to school for a time
wrestling: ['resliŋ] a sport in which two people try to throw each other to the ground

as the last pupil came in, Jamie began at once explaining the details of the plan. There was no time to lose.

When he was sure that everyone knew exactly what to do, Jamie leaned forward and looked at each of them. He reminded them that the job they had to do was dangerous. If the Snakeman or any of his gang saw what was going on, there would be a fight and people would get hurt. But whatever happened, it was the job of the bodyguards to make sure that nothing stopped the sale of the newspapers. When he finished talking, everyone in the group nodded. Then, like the captain of a team, Jamie put his hands on the table and the others all put their hands around his. "Each of us knows what to do. The staff members go directly to their positions in the halls, the others come with me. OK, guys, let's do it!" he cried. "Let's do it!" cried the others. Immediately, they left the room the same way they had come in, one by one.

Meanwhile, a large white *delivery van* had just pulled up in the parking area behind the cafeteria. A man got out, opened the side door of the van and went inside. At that moment, Jamie came around the corner. Seeing the van, he *scanned* the parking area to make sure that no one was watching. Then he gave a little signal to the others, who were waiting behind the corner.

When they reached the van, the man inside came out carrying a large package. He gave it to Jamie and told the others to go in one at a time and pick up their packages. Then, led by Jamie, they *marched* back into

delivery van: a vehicle like a large car used for carrying goods
to scan: to look at every part of sth carefully
to march: to walk somewhere quickly in a determined way

the school carrying the packages. A few minutes later, the scene repeated itself with Jamie again leading the way.

Jamie looked at his watch. Two more minutes to the bell. Everything was ready. The six newspaper stands were set up, and at each of them a staff member with a bodyguard was in place. He looked down the hall at Cathy and flashed her the victory sign. She flashed it back. Just then, the bell rang. The next half hour was *chaotic*. The newspaper stands were surrounded by pupils pushing and shouting and holding money in their hands. By the time the bell rang for the start of the afternoon classes, the special issue of The Beacon was gone, every single copy had been sold!

Later that afternoon there was a *knock* at the door in the middle of Mr. Ferrero's Spanish class. Heads *snapped around*. "Are Jamie Hanson and Cathy Crosby here? They're wanted in the principal's office at once!" Jamie and Cathy had been expecting this, so they weren't surprised, but the class was and Mr. Ferrero had a hard time quieting them down again after the two had left the room. On their way down the long corridor to the principal's office, they didn't say a word. Noticing that Jamie looked a little pale, Cathy tried to smile at him, but a smile wouldn't come.

chaotic: [keɪˈɒtɪk] without any order
knock: the sound of sb hitting the door
to snap around: to move or turn around very quickly

58

16

Dr. Callahan was standing behind his desk waiting for them. Beside him sat Ms. Southerland, looking even angrier than the principal. On the desk lay a copy of the special issue of The Beacon. After a long moment of silence in which Dr. Callahan glared at Jamie and 5 Ms. Southerland at Cathy, Dr. Callahan cleared his throat.

"What have you got to say to this, young man?" he said suddenly, pointing at the newspaper on his desk. His voice shook with anger.

Jamie hesitated, searching for the right words. "It all
5 started –"

"I can explain everything –" Cathy cut in, but suddenly Ms. Southerland shot up from her seat.

"Sit down, young woman, and don't speak another word unless you are spoken to!" she hissed. Cathy
10 glared at her, but sat down.

"Now, as I was saying before we were *interrupted*, what is the meaning of this?" Dr. Callahan picked up the newspaper and shook it in Jamie's face. "Who gave you permission to print this? Did Ms. Southerland give
15 you permission? Did I give you permission? WHO WAS IT?" His voice had gone from loud to very loud.

Just then, the phone rang.

"But Judy, didn't I say no calls for the next 10 minutes! Who? The *mayor*? *For God's sake*, put him through." As if
20 by magic, the angry look on Dr. Callahan's face suddenly turned into a warm smile. He stood up and went over to the window, his back to the others.

"Hello, Dr. Callahan speaking. ..Hello, Mayor Simpson, how are you? ...What can I do for you, mayor? I
25 know you're a busy man...What???" Dr. Callahan's voice suddenly became thin and nervous. "No, that's not true... of course, I knew about it...I know, I know...it's *terrible*, just terrible...yes, as soon as I found out I went into

---

interrupted: forced to pause or stop
mayor: [meə] the head of the government of a town or city
for God's sake: said to emphasize that it is important to do sth
terrible: very unpleasant, making you feel very unhappy, upset or frightened

60

action...You're absolutely right, a situation like that cannot be *tolerated*...exactly my words, yes...no, no it was all planned...top secret, it had to be...What? ...Mrs. Crosby needn't have done that...no, no, that wasn't necessary at all...I had *arranged* to have a copy brought to you personally as soon as The Beacon came out...yes, yes, the police have been informed...I know it's an election year...don't worry, everything is under control...We'll have this cleaned up within a few days...you have my word, Mayor Simpson.. The two reporters? They're sitting right here in my office...of course I'll tell them...yes, yes, I will.. this evening?...Who? ...right, we'll be there... nice talking to you, Mayor... goodbye...yes, yes, I promise...we'll take care of everything...you can depend on me. See you at the press conference...goodbye."

Dr. Callahan remained standing at the window, not moving. When he finally turned around, Cathy was surprised at the change in him. On the phone he had been all smiles, now he stood facing them looking very serious. He began slowly. "This won't be easy for me, but I *owe* you an explanation, and I'm going to give you one. What you're probably asking yourselves is: why would Dr. Callahan want to cover up the Snakeman story? Why wasn't he happy that the truth came out? You might well be thinking that I have been somehow involved in this whole business." He paused, his eyes searching theirs. "Well, I haven't!" His eyes continued to search theirs, looking for a some kind of a reaction. "But of course I do know what goes on in my school. I

tolerated: accepted
to arrange: to plan or organize sth
to owe: to feel that you ought to do sth for sb or give them sth

61

keep my eyes and ears open. I have been hearing things about a gang at Portland High for the past year or so. But instead of looking into it, I didn't do anything about it. And that was a big *mistake*. It's probably
5 very difficult for you to understand that, but let me try to explain." He cleared his throat. Cathy noticed that drops of *sweat* had formed on the top of his hairless head and were beginning to run down his face. "Being the principal of a large school like Portland High isn't
10 always easy. In the past twenty years there have been good times, but we've also been through some difficult times. And now, after 20 years, in my final year and looking forward to my *retirement*, I didn't want to have to deal with any more crises. That was wrong. It was
15 wrong to be thinking of myself instead of the pupils, especially those like you, Cathy, victims of the Snakeman." Dr. Callahan paused and took a deep breath. "You're probably saying to yourselves that I am only talking this way because I have to, because of the
20 phone call from Mayor Simpson. That's only partly true. I'm going to take action to stop the Snakeman because I want to, because I realize that my past behavior was wrong and because I want to do what is right from now on." Again he fixed his eyes on theirs, look-
25 ing for a positive reaction.

   Just then, Ms. Southerland stood up. "I've got something to say, too," she said. "This isn't easy for me, either. But what Dr. Callahan has just said has helped me to know what is right. Together with the principal,

mistake: an action or an opinion that is not correct
sweat: [swet] drops on your skin when you are hot, nervous, etc.
retirement: that time of life after you no longer have to work

I wanted to cover up the truth about the Snakeman, and when you brought out your front-page story in The Beacon, I was shocked and very, very angry. I wanted Dr. Callahan to punish you. I've always thought that it was best for our school when only good news got into our school newspaper. If something bad happened in the school, I did my best to keep it out of the newspaper. I thought that that would help make Portland High a better school than the others. Now I see how wrong I was and I'm very sorry about it. I can only ask you to try to understand and perhaps *forgive* me." Ms. Southerland sat down again slowly.

There was a moment of silence. Cathy could have said something, but she felt that it was better to wait and give everyone, especially Dr. Callahan and Ms. Southerland, the chance to think about what had just been said. She was happy that they had realized their mistake and she didn't want to make things too easy for them by talking too soon. Jamie sat thinking, too – the same thoughts? But finally, he broke the silence. "It's okay, you don't have to say you're sorry. We understand, don't we, Cath?" Cathy nodded her head.

Dr. Callahan jumped up from his seat like a man who had just been freed from prison. He came around the desk quickly, followed by Ms. Southerland, and they both shook Cathy's and Jamie's hands, saying 'thank you' again and again.

When the principal had his feelings under control again, he cleared his throat. "Now that we are a, uh, team," he began, "it's time we got organized. First of all,

---

to forgive: to stop feeling angry with sb who has done sth to harm or upset you

I want to tell you what the mayor said. He read your front-page story and called to say how pleased he was that we have brought this bad situation out into the open." Cathy winked at Jamie when Dr. Callahan
5 emphasized the word 'we'. "When I said that the authors of the story were sitting right here, he told me to congratulate you on your *courageous* piece of reporting and said that he was looking forward to meeting you personally. He says that he's arranged a press con-
10 ference for 7 o'clock this evening at the city hall and wants all of us to be there. You will come, won't you?" he said, looking intently at Cathy and Jamie. They nodded.

"As I said, Mayor Simpson was very pleased and
15 impressed that, uh, we have managed to expose this bad situation at our school, and it is his wish that the Snakeman and his gang be *expelled* from Portland High as soon as possible. I promised him that we would act quickly. Of course, we will need your help. In your
20 story you wrote that any victim of the Snakeman gang or any pupil or teacher who knows anything about them, should get in touch with you. I would be thankful if you passed any information you get along to me. We need to get a clear picture of the gang's activities
25 to help the police with their investigation."

When Jamie said they would, Dr. Callahan seemed pleased. But then he hesitated, and it was apparent to Cathy that what he was going to say next wasn't easy for him. "I'm sure that I speak for Ms. Southerland,
30 too, when I say how thankful we are for what you've

courageous: [kə'reɪdʒəs] fearless
expelled: to be officially made to leave

64

done for Portland High. If you hadn't been so coura- geous, the situation would have grown worse and worse. We are very proud of you." He glanced over at Ms. Southerland.

"Very proud," she said, smiling.   5

"Right now it's important to ...uh...*practice* what we are going to say at the mayor's press conference. I'm sure you'll agree that we should try...um...to make a good impression. I suggest that I speak first, followed by Ms. Southerland – you will prepare a short statement,   10 won't you, Francis?" Dr. Callahan smiled at her.

"Of course," she said immediately.

"Good," he said, turning back to Jamie and Cathy. "And after we've had our say, it will be your turn. It's...um...very important that our statements ...uh...all   15 fit together well." He laughed nervously. "You know how reporters can be sometimes – like dogs after a bone. If they think something is not exactly right, they start asking all kinds of questions. And that can be very unpleasant." Dr. Callahan paused, as if he was remem- 20 bering an experience like that.

"Are you ready for our little 'practice press confer- ence'?"

"Ready!" Cathy and Jamie said at the same time.

"You, too, Francis?"   25

"Ready!"

"OK," said Dr. Callahan with a happy grin, "let's get started: LIGHTS, CAMERA, ACTION!"

---

to practice: to do sth again and again in order to be able to do it better

17

When the police came for the Snakeman, he had disappeared. He wasn't in school or at home or anywhere else in the city. He must have left town as soon as he heard about the front-page story in The Beacon.

5   In the following weeks, Cathy and Jamie were often spoken to by pupils who had been on the Snakeman's list. They were, of course, *relieved* that he was gone, but many of them said that the fear of him remained. The Snakeman was gone, but in a very real way he was still
10 there, still following them, even in their dreams. Cathy knew exactly what they meant. In long discussions with Jamie, she had begun to get her fear under control, but it was still strong in her. When she was talking about these things with her mother one
15 evening, Eileen gave her the idea of forming a group. She said that the best way to deal with the problem – 'The Snakeman *Syndrome*' as Cathy called it – was to talk about their experience with the Snakeman and face their fears by admitting them and discussing them
20 openly.

Cathy took her mom's advice. With Jamie's help, she got the group started. Eileen said that they could meet at their house. In the beginning there were only a handful of pupils who came, but after a few weeks the
25 number had grown to over twenty. The first meetings

relieved: [rɪˈliːvd] feeling happy
syndrome: [ˈsɪndrəʊm] a set of symptoms of certain diseases or medical problems

didn't go well, with almost no one wanting to say much. But after a while, encouraged by the good example of Cathy and a few others, more and more of the pupils began to talk about their experience and their feelings. In fact, it seemed at times that everyone wanted to talk at once, and sometimes the meetings got a little out of control.

Yet they were working. Cathy could tell from the laughter. There had been none in the beginning, but from week to week the laughter had grown stronger and stronger. In the first weeks, there was an atmosphere of fear in the room. You could see it in the faces. You could almost touch it. But little by little that atmosphere had changed, slowly but surely turning into a freer, happier mood. Looking around at the smiling faces, Cathy was proud of the pupils there. She knew what they had gone through. It wasn't easy to talk about such bad experiences, but they had done it. In a group in which everyone shared the same experience, they had found the strength to talk about their fears and, in that way, to start *overcoming* them.

Cathy had talked about her fears, too, and she had managed to overcome some of them, but not the strongest fear of all: that the Snakeman would come one day and take revenge on her. But when she talked about that, Jamie would say that if he returned, he would be coming for both of them. After all, he said, both of them had signed their names to that front-page story. But Cathy knew in her heart that the Snakeman had a special reason for coming after her: in his way he

to overcome: to deal with a problem successfully

had liked her, had wanted her to be his girl, and then she had let him down. Jamie told her not to worry, he was there, he would protect her, etc. etc. But, of course, when it came down to it, he wouldn't be there. The Snakeman would strike when she was alone, not when Jamie was with her.

And so the fear remained. She didn't talk about it anymore, but when she was alone she felt it. Sometimes she thought she saw him – in a crowd, or in a passing car – and the fear would strike her heart again. Those who knew Cathy well – Ophir, Jamie and her mother – noticed the change in her, how nervous she had become, but they were unable to help her. Nothing they said could make Cathy stop worrying.

The final meeting of the group was a party. There was good food and good music – Jamie was DJ for the evening – and before long, everyone was laughing and having a good time. Everyone except Cathy, who couldn't get into the party spirit. Just then, Ophir arrived, out of breath and carrying a newspaper under her arm. She went straight across the room to Jamie and pointed to something in the newspaper. He read for a moment, then looked at Ophir and nodded. Together they went over to Cathy, who was standing in a corner talking to her mother.

"Hi Eileen, hi Cath. Excuse us, but Ophir just showed me something we think Cathy should read," Jamie said, holding up the newspaper.

"Hey, The Boston Globe – what's this all about?"

"Just read this," he said, opening the paper and pointing at an article.

"OK, OK." Cathy held up the newspaper and read.

Portland youth killed in drug *bust*

Gordon Baker, an 18-year-old *resident* of Portland, Maine, died shortly after being taken to Boston General Hospital last night. Mr. Baker, whom the police had been watching for some time, was observed yesterday selling drugs to school children. When *Officers* Jessica Jordan and Orwell Jackson moved in to make the arrest, Baker suddenly pulled a gun and ran. Ordered to stop, he turned and started shooting at the officers, who shot back. In the gun fight that followed, Jackson was hit in the arm. Baker was hit twice in the chest and fell to the ground. Both men were taken to the hospital immediately.

Cathy sat down and put her head in her hands. Her whole body began to shake. She was crying silently. Eileen, Jamie and Ophir looked at each other. Jamie was about to say something when Eileen held up her hand, a signal that meant: let her cry. The three of them remained standing there for several minutes, waiting. Finally, when the crying had almost stopped, Eileen put her hands on her daughter's shoulders. Cathy looked up and tried to smile.

"I...don't know...what...to say," she *whispered*.

"It's okay, Cath, you don't have to say anything. Everything's going to be alright from now on," Eileen said.

---

bust (infl): an unexpected visit made by the police in order to arrest people
resident: a person who lives in a certain place
officer (AE): what a policeman is often called
to whisper: ['wɪspə] to say sth very quietly

Cathy looked at the three of them, from one to the other, nodding slowly. "I think so. Yeah, everything is going to be alright."

She got up and put her arms around her mother, then around Ophir and then, for the longest time, around Jamie.

Questions

There are three questions for each chapter. Question 1 is a pre-reading question. Question 2 deals with the content of the chapter and you should answer this while your are reading it or immediately after having read it. Question 3 should be answered after you have read the chapter – possibly as a homework assignment in writing.

Chapter 1

1. Your family has moved to another city. It's your first day at your new school. What are the thoughts and feelings you wake up with on the morning of your first day?

2. Why did Cathy like Jamie?
   Do you think Jamie likes Cathy?

3. Think through two or three possible ways the relationship between Jamie and Cathy might develop.

Chapter 2

1. Think about what you would do if a gang told you that you would have to hand over half your pocket money every week.

2. Say what you think of the way Cathy reacts when surrounded by the Snakeman and his gang.

3. Think about how Cathy might act in the dangerous situation she's now in. What could she do?

Chapter 3

1. If you got into a dangerous situation would you talk to your parents about it? Tell why you would, or wouldn't.

2. Do you think Cathy's decision not to tell her mother about it was right? Try to think of arguments for and against her decision.

3. What do you think might be the strategy she is going to follow in the beginning?

Chapter 4

1. Do you think that Cathy's strategy of non-resistance will work in the long run?

2. What do you think of Cathy's new strategy?

3. What do you think will be the result of Cathy's search for people she can trust?

Chapter 5

1. Think of different ways the principal might react when Cathy talks to him about her 'problem'.

2. Say what you think is making the principal so nervous during his talk with Cathy.

3. What role will the principal play in the rest of the story? Will he try to stop Cathy?

Chapter 6

1. How would you go about trying to find out who you can trust? What kinds of questions would you ask?

2. What made Cathy so sure that Mr. Black couldn't be trusted?

3. What thoughts might be going through Cathy's mind after talking with Dr. Callahan and Mr. Black?

Chapter 7

1. How do you think Cathy's mother's will react when Cathy tells her about the Snakeman?

2. Describe how Eileen reacted to what her daughter had told her, and say what you think of her reaction.

3. What might Eileen's thoughts be about Cathy's situation in the days following their talk?

Chapter 8

1. Jamie is taking Cathy on a canoeing trip for the day. Imagine what the trip might be like. Describe a scene that could possibly take place.

2. Describe some of the highlights of the trip.

3. Using the references to what she wrote in her diary about the trip, fill in the rest.

Chapter 9

1. Imagine that the Snakeman wants Cathy to be his girl and that he is putting her under pressure to say yes. Think about how Cathy would act in that kind of situation.

2. Describe in a summary way how she reacted to the Snakeman's pressure, and say what you think of her reaction.

3. Develop some ideas about what kind of plan Cathy has made.

Chapter 10

1. Imagine that Cathy dreamed about the Snakeman's plan to make her his girl. Describe the dream you think she might have had.

2. Try to interpret Cathy's dream. What does it mean? How is it related to what she experienced that day, when she talked with the Snakeman?

3. Ask yourself whether the dream will help or hinder Cathy in trying to carry out her plan.

Chapter 11

1. Try to imagine what it's like when your best friend doesn't want to help you when you are in trouble.

2. Describe Jamie's behavior in this scene, and say what you think of it.

3. Say what thoughts you think go through Jamie's head after his talk with Cathy.

Chapter 12

1. Try to imagine what the faculty adviser says to Cathy when she brings up her idea of using the school newspaper for a front-page story about the Snakeman and his gang.

2. Explain why Cathy is so angry with Jamie when she walks out.

3. Ask yourself what will become of the relationship between Jamie and Cathy after this. Think about possible developments in the story.

Chapter 13

1. Imagine that Cathy went out with the Snakeman in order to make Jamie jealous. Say how she might describe the date to Jamie afterward.

2. Explain how Cathy uses the date to make Jamie jealous.

3. Try to imagine the scene in which Jamie tries to make Ms. Southerland realize that she must let them print their story about the Snakeman in The Beacon.

Chapter 14

1. Ask yourself what Jamie might do when Ms. Southerland says that she will not give permission to use the school newspaper for their story.

2. Trace Cathy's changing moods in this scene. Say what you think of the way she reacts to the good news about the special issue.

3. Imagine the difficulties Jamie and Cathy have to face in order to bring out the special edition. Try to think how they could overcome these difficulties and bring out the newspaper successfully.

Chapter 15

1. Imagine a conversation between Cathy and Jamie that takes place the evening before the day of the special 'Snakeman issue' of The Beacon.

2. Describe the role Jamie plays in this scene and comment on how well he carries it out.

3. Imagine what happens at the meeting between Jamie and Cathy and the principal.

Chapter 16

1. Imagine what could happen to make the principal decide to side with Cathy and Jamie.

2. Why does Dr. Callahan say that he is going to take action to stop the Snakeman?

3. (in group work) Prepare the four statements (Dr. Callahan's, Ms. Southerland's, Cathy's and Jamie's), so that they all fit together well.

Chapter 17

1. Think about what life would be like for Cathy if the police weren't able to catch the Snakeman.

2. Try to explain why Cathy wasn't able to catch the spirit of the party.

3. Can you imagine a good ending to the story in which the Snakeman isn't killed?

Working with grammar

Dear Pupil: if you've forgotten the rules for CONDITIONAL (IF) SENTENCES and INDIRECT SPEECH, look them up or ask your teacher for help.

Part I: If sentences

1) CONDITIONAL I
(use if + present tense – will future)

1   If Cathy (try) to run away, the gang (catch) her.

2   If Cathy (pay) the Snakeman every week,
    she (not get) into trouble.

3   Mrs. Crosby (want) to help, if Cathy (let) her.

4   If Jamie (ask) her to go with him, Cathy (say) yes.

5   Jamie and Cathy (be able) to watch the moose
    from up close, if they (keep) quiet.

6   If you (make) Dr. Callahan nervous, he (start)
    pulling on his tie.

7   Ms. Southerland (stop) a story getting into the
    school newspaper if she (think) it's too negative.

2) CONDITIONAL II
(use if + past tense – would/could)

1   I (be) very frightened if someone like the Snakeman (tell) me to give him money.

2   If I (be) Cathy, I (do) the same things she did.

3   If a boy like Jamie (ask) you to go canoeing, your parents (let) you go?

4   If your principal (be) like Dr. Callahan, you (dislike) him?

5   If I (be) Cathy, I (tell) my mother not to move so often.

6   If a guy like the Snakeman (ask) me to go for a chopper ride with him, I (say) no!

3) CONDITIONAL III
(use if + past perfect – would have/could have)

1   If Cathy (not be) such an outdoor girl, she (not enjoy) the canoeing trip so much.

2   If Cathy and Jamie (not get) so cold wading in the river, there (not be) a "tickle Party".

3   If Cathy (not have) the courage to go out with the Snakeman, Jamie (not agree) to side with her against Ms. Southerland.

4 The Snakeman (make) Cathy his partner if only she (want) that.

5 If the Snakeman (not leave) town quickly, the police (catch) him.

6 Cathy (be) a lot happier if she (not be) certain that the Snakeman would return to get her.

Part II: Indirect Speech

1) INDIRECT SPEECH (AFFIRMATIVE SENTENCES)

Here are some things Cathy (might have) said to her mother. Change the direct speech into indirect speech.

1 "A gang at school wants me to give them money every week."

2 "I'm going to try to find people I can trust."

3 "I know at least two other pupils who are victims of the gang."

4 "I think the best way to deal with the problem is just to give them the money."

5 "I'll keep you informed of what happens."

6 "You don't have to worry about me."

2) INDIRECT SPEECH (INSTRUCTIONS, ORDERS)

Here are some things the Snakeman (might have) said to Cathy. Change the direct speech into indirect speech.

1 "Don't try to scream!"

2 "Do exactly as I say."

3 "You must meet me at the same time and the same place every week."

4 "Give me your necklace or I'll tear it from your neck!"

5 "Don't you ever think of telling others about me!"

6 "Show me your tattoo!"

3) INDIRECT SPEECH (QUESTIONS)

Here are some things Cathy (might have) asked Jamie about their canoeing trip. Change the direct speech into indirect speech.

1 "Where are we going?"

2 "What do I have to bring with me?"

3 "When do you want me to be ready?"

4 "Why do I have to leave my cell phone at home?"

5   "Will we be home by six?"

6   "Are you taking a camera with you?"

Suggested Answers

Part I: If Sentences, Condition I

1 If Cathy tries to run away, the gang will catch her.
2 If Cathy pays the Snakeman every week, she will not get into trouble.
3 Mrs. Crosby will want to help if Cathy lets her.
4 If Jamie asks her to go with him, Cathy will say yes.
5 Jamie and Cathy will be able to watch the moose from up close if they keep quiet.
6 If you make Dr. Callahan nervous, he will start pulling on his tie.
7 Ms. Southerland will stop a story getting into the school newspaper if she thinks it is too negative.

2) Conditional II

1 I would be very frightened if someone like the Snakeman told me to give him money.
2 If I was (were) Cathy, I would do the same things she did.
3 If a boy like Jamie asked you to go canoeing with him, would your parents let you go?
4 If your principal was (were) like Dr. Callahan, would you dislike him?
5 If I was (were) Cathy, I would tell my mother not to move so often.
6 If a guy like the Snakeman asked me to go for a chopper ride with him, I would say no!

3) Conditional III

1 If Cathy hadn't been such an outdoor girl, she wouldn't have enjoyed the canoeing trip so much.

2   If Cathy and Jamie hadn't gotten so cold wading in the river, there wouldn't have been a "tickle party".

3   If Cathy hadn't had the courage to go out with the Snakeman, Jamie wouldn't have agreed to side with her against Ms. Southerland.

4   The Snakeman would have made Cathy his partner if only she had wanted that.

5   If the Snakeman hadn't left town quickly, the police would have caught him.

6   Cathy would have been a lot happier if she hadn't been certain that the Snakeman would return to get her.

Part II: Indirect Speech

1) Indirect Speech (Affirmative Sentences)

1   Cathy told her mother that a gang at school wanted her to give them money every week.

2   Cathy said that she was going to try to find people she could trust.

3   She said (pointed out) that she knew at least two other pupils who were victims of the gang.

4   She said (explained) that she thought the best way to deal with the problem was just to give them the money.

5   Cathy said (promised) that she would keep her informed.

6   Cathy said (added) that she didn't have to worry about her.

2) Indirect Speech (Instructions, Orders)

1 The Snakeman warned Cathy not to try to scream.
2 He told (warned) her to do exactly as he said.
3 He told her to meet him at the same time and the same place every week.
4 He told (ordered) her to give him her necklace or he would tear it from her neck.
5 He warned her not to ever think of telling others about him.
6 He told (ordered) her to show him her tattoo.

3) Indirect Speech (Questions)

1 Cathy asked Jamie where they were going.
2 She wanted to know what she had to bring with her.
3 She asked him when he wanted her to be ready.
4 She wanted to know why she had to leave her cell phone at home.
5 She asked him if (whether) they would be home by six.
6 She wanted to know if he was taking a camera with him.